To:

From:

For Mike and Seda, Zooey and Blueberry, Ada and Hedgie,
and for my own Big Bird.
—EG

For my niece Sungah, nephew Luah, and my family
who encourage me with endless love.
—SL

Published by Sourcebooks Wonderland, an imprint of Sourcebooks Kids
P.O. Box 4410, Naperville, Illinois 60567–4410
(630) 961-3900
sourcebookskids.com

Cataloging-in-Publication Data is on file with the Library of Congress.

Source of Production: Phoenix Color, Hagerstown, Maryland, United States of America
Date of Production: November 2021
Run Number: 5023616

Printed and bound in the United States of America.
PHC 10 9 8 7 6 5 4 3 2 1

Little Blue Bunny

words by **Erin Guendelsberger**
pictures by **Stila Lim**

sourcebooks
wonderland

Even on that very first day, the little blue bunny knew something wonderful was about to happen.

The bunny arrived at the house on a warm afternoon in spring, the boy's birthday. It was a day full of paper and ribbons, of cake and candles, of singing and laughter.

And waiting inside a bright green box was the little blue bunny.

Immediately, the boy loved the bunny with its long floppy ears, soft blue fur, and pink velvet nose. And immediately, the bunny loved the boy.

When the boy had gone to bed that night, carried upstairs already asleep and placed beneath the covers, the bunny was set on a shelf in his bedroom.

"Welcome," an orange, rubber dinosaur said to the bunny. The other toys welcomed the bunny, as well—a spiny-soft hedgehog, a dump truck, a calico kitten, and more.

"Thank you!" said Blue Bunny. "I like this place very much, but I truly can't wait to go on adventures. There's so much I want to do!"

"The boy will take you places," purred the calico kitten.

"Oh, but I'm not talking about doing *little things*," said Blue Bunny. "I'm talking about *great big things*... The kind of adventures I'll have on my own when the boy grows up and doesn't need me anymore."

"I know my job right now is to be the best friend I can be," said Blue Bunny. "But one day...

"I want to explore! I'll see
the tallest skyscrapers...

and sail the
seas searching
for treasure.

I'll journey to
the hidden depths
of exotic jungles.

I'll sleep beneath the canopy of a million stars."

"I have important things to do!" said the bunny. "I just want to be…special."

"Ah, little one," said a new voice. Blue Bunny noticed for the first time a brown teddy bear sitting next to him. The bear had limp ears, worn fur, and a tail that looked as though it had fallen off and been stitched back on again.

Bear smiled. "You have many adventures to come, and perhaps sooner than you think."

"I'm ready!" said the little blue bunny.

The next morning, the boy pulled Blue Bunny down from the shelf. He hugged the bunny close and rubbed the bunny's soft fur against his cheeks. They had lots of big plans.

They built tall towers…and interesting houses…and colorful roads.

Dump Truck *vroom-vroomed* around the landscape.

Blue Bunny *hop-hopped* down the road, exploring the city and meeting new people.

At the end of the day, the bunny felt tired and happy, falling asleep in the boy's arms, and wondering what exciting things they would find tomorrow.

The next day, the boy and the bunny braved the waves to track infamous pirates.

They watched the pirate captain's red-winged companion flit and fly through the sky and perch high above them.

Then they discovered buried treasure—precious gems jagged or smooth, large or teeny tiny—that filled their pockets to the brim. Smiles never-ending.

After that, it seemed as though the boy and the bunny were never apart—from the *splish-splash* of spring and *sizzle* of summer, to the *crunch-crunch* of fall and the *crackle* of winter.

Blue Bunny loved the boy and all the fun they had together, but sometimes wondered about growing up to do something spectacular and important, those *great big things*.

Even so, the bunny was always there when needed most.

The Christmas that the boy got sick, Blue Bunny cuddled up with him as the boy's parents came and went.

When the boy was anxious about his first day of school, the bunny never left his side.

When the boy's best friend moved away, Blue Bunny offered soft ears to dry the boy's tears.

And when the boy was happy—oh, what joy! They danced and laughed. They imagined and created.

Blue Bunny and the boy shared a magical world they built one day at a time.

As the boy grew older, their adventures got bigger.

They explored a conservatory and marveled at wild plants and curious reptiles from faraway lands.

They went on sleepovers and had such great fun with so many friends! They played and joked and laughed until their sides ached.

They went on a long car trip, driving all the way to the ocean. Out the window, Blue Bunny saw everything they passed.

They stopped to camp and slept in a tent with the top open, looking up at a sky filled with twinkling stars. The boy hugged the bunny close against the chilly night air.

Days turned into weeks, weeks into months, and months into years. Still, the boy kept the bunny nearby.

One morning, the boy woke up and held the bunny out at arm's length, staring at its worn fur, limp ears, and tattered tail. The boy put Blue Bunny under his arm and walked down the stairs. Were they going out for their next adventure?

The boy found his mom in the laundry room and handed Blue Bunny to her. The bunny was suddenly worried. What was happening?

And then with deep sadness, the bunny remembered that once, long ago, the boy had handed a broken car to his mom. She had said it couldn't be fixed.

So, did this mean the boy and the bunny already had their last adventure? Blue Bunny sighed as the boy walked away.

The boy's mom picked up Blue Bunny and set to work, reaching into a cabinet for a small kit full of needles and thread, fabric and buttons.

She washed the bunny's dirty fur and put the bunny into the dryer to tumble round and round. She stuffed, she sewed, she snipped, and she smoothed. Once she was all done, she set the bunny on the boy's bed.

When the boy returned after school, he hugged the bunny close and rubbed the newly soft fur against his cheeks. The bunny had never felt so whole, so special.

For the boy still loved the bunny. And the bunny still loved the boy.

One evening, the boy was away, as he often was those days. Blue Bunny sat on the shelf beside the brown teddy bear. They were good friends after all this time.

"So," said Bear, "What will tomorrow hold?"

"I'm not sure," said Blue Bunny. "Sometimes I feel like I've done everything there is to do already. I suppose all of my dreams have come true!"

And just like that, the little blue bunny understood. The bunny hadn't needed to wait for the boy to grow up in order to do something amazing. All of their adventures, even the smallest ones, were incredible and important because they were right here. *Together.*

Soon, the boy was a young man, but he
kept the bunny close while he...
studied for exams,
made big decisions,
and asked even bigger questions.

When the boy was fully grown, his forever friend was never forgotten. Blue Bunny still had a place in his home and his heart for every *great big thing*, always there to comfort, to listen, or simply, to wait.

...And one day, a new baby arrived.

Blue Bunny looked at the child, bright eyes and curious hands, and thought about the many adventures to come.

"I'm ready!" said the little blue bunny.